SEA TURTLE'S JOURNEY

Written and Illustrated by Eleanor A. Hutton

D1404200

Published by PRGOTT BOOKS

P.O. Box 43, Norway, Maine 04268

WWW.PRGOTTBOOKS.NET

SEA TURTLE'S JOURNEY

Written and Illustrated by Eleanor A. Hutton
Layout by Laura Ashton

ISBN 978-0-9845898-3-8

Published by **PRGott Books**, P.O. Box 43, Norway, ME 04268

Printed in the United States of America

Dedicated to my mother Marjorie M. Hutton
and my husband Douglas E. Kidd

SEA TURTLE'S JOURNEY

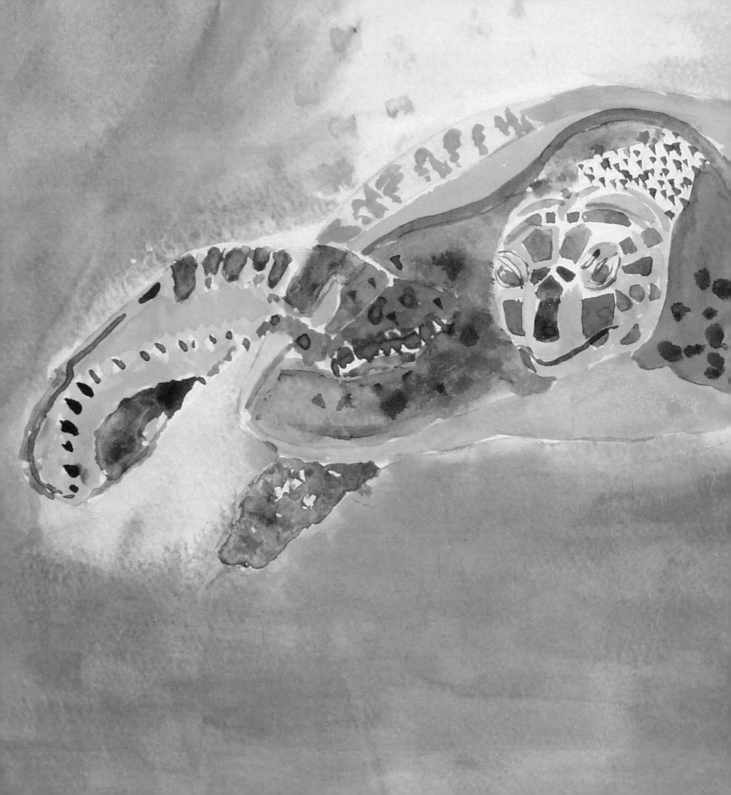

The midnight turtle
wore a mantle of blue
from the sea's edge.

It had been forever, she thought, as she rolled over a wave.

The evening's cool hand
demanded nothing of her.

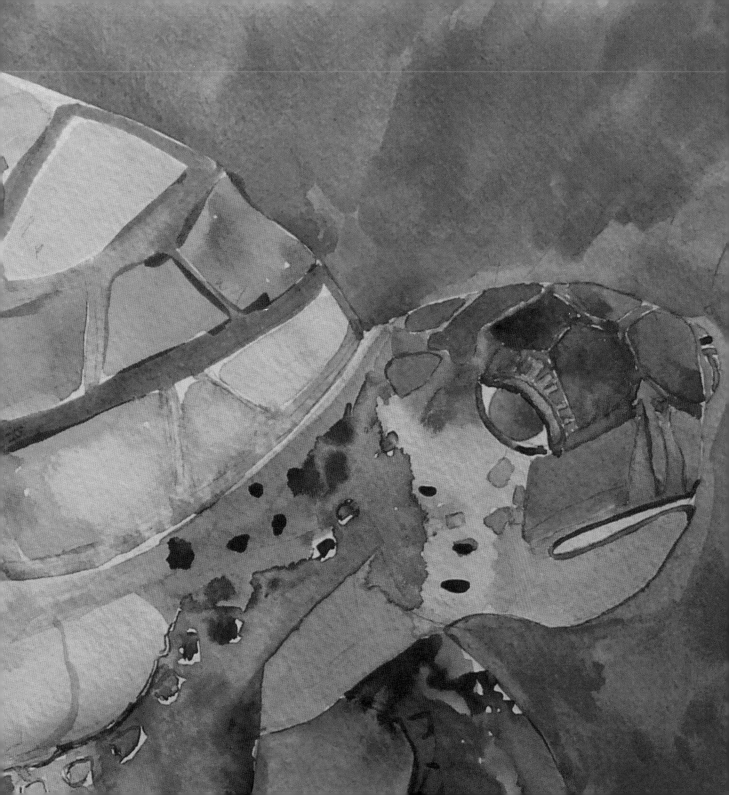

She saw the beach
glittering with shells.

She shed seaweed ribbons
as she played in the waves.

Nearby she saw a shell,
whole,
opened,
with a pearl.

Under the
yellow moon
she swam ...

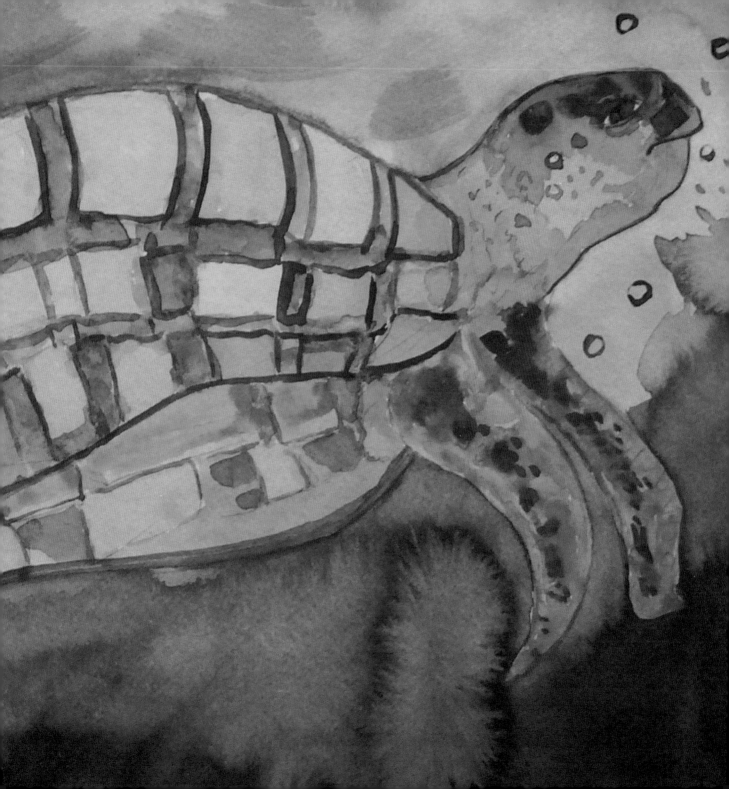

to the ocean's shore.

There she laid her eggs,
burying them in the sand
as she sang of
moon jewels,
early pearls,
and late jades.

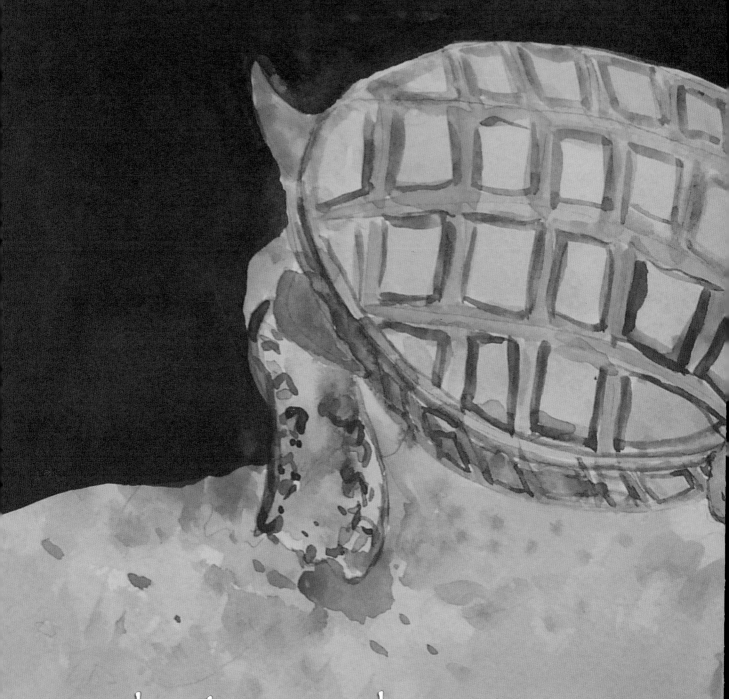

She dove in the water.

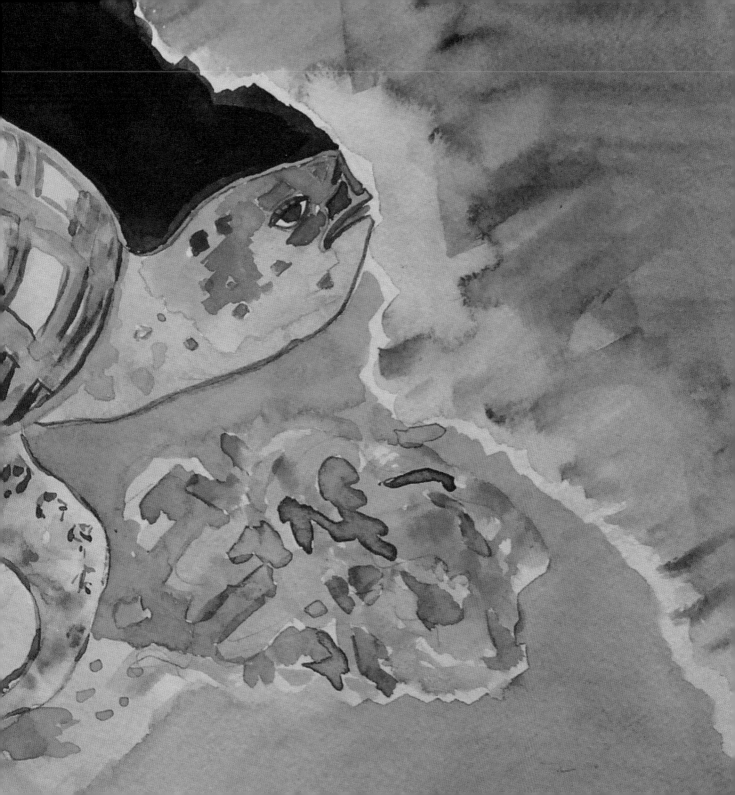

and up again through the blue.

As she surfaced, she saw
two rings of stars—apart,

then together—the promise of a new day to come.

In the starlight, she saw the seven baby turtles finding their way across the beach to the ocean.

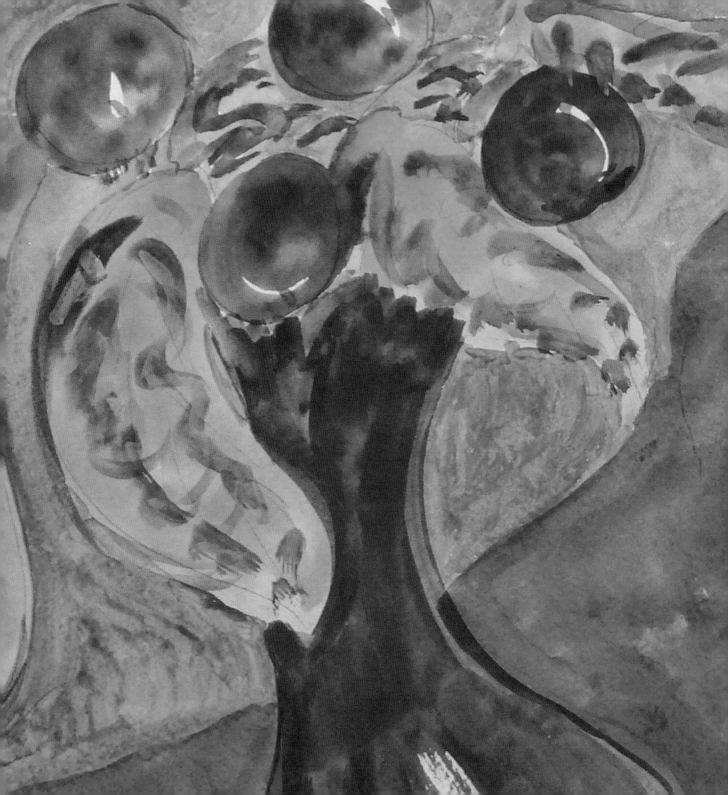

She swam ahead,
past an old palm tree.

Quickly,
under the moon,
the little turtles
caught the tide and
rode behind the
mama turtle,

chanting of
moon jewels,
early pearls,
and late jades.

The End

If you liked *Sea Turtle's Journey*, with its lovely illustrations,
you will also enjoy the Helium Books, a children's series
illustrated by Eleanor A. Hutton and written by E.Dorinda Shelley.

The Helium Egg and *The Helium Table*, as well as
Sea Turtle's Journey, can be found on Amazon.com,
and on www.norasbooknook.com

www.norasbooknook.com

6754098R0

Made in the USA
Charleston, SC
04 December 2010